My Friends

Written by
Marcia Vaughan

Illustrated by
Anni Matsick

📖 ScottForesman
A Division of HarperCollins*Publishers*

Come and meet my friends.

I like to play a ball game
with Mario.

3

I like to play a string game
with Tonya.

I like to play a stone game
with Sothie.

I like to play a hand game
with Tameo.

I like to play soccer
with Juan.

And my friends all like to play baseball with me.